A LIFT-THE-FLAP BOOK

Emily and Her Daddy

1st Fathers Day
2003

Claire Masurel • Illustrated by Susan Calitri

PUFFIN BOOKS

Today is Emily and Daddy's special day.

"We're going to have a great time, just the two of us," says Daddy.

"Bye, Mom!
Bye, Leo!"

At the park, Emily and
Daddy go for a boat ride.

"The ducks are following us!"

Emily shares some popcorn.

"Let's go watch the baseball game, Emily."

"Here's a good place
for a picnic," says Daddy.

"Can you teach me how to hit a home run, Daddy?"

"Look! The balloon man."

Back home, Emily tells Mom about her day with Daddy.

"We had so much fun!"

Emily loves her daddy.
And Daddy loves Emily.